Smithsonian

Dig It:
Ocean
Treasures

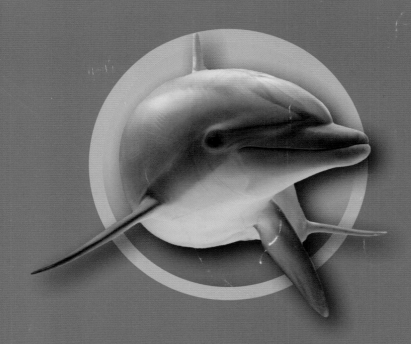

Emily Rose Oachs

Silver Dolphin Books

An imprint of Printers Row Publishing Group
10350 Barnes Canyon Road, Suite 100, San Diego, CA 92121
www.silverdolphinbooks.com

Printers Row Publishing Group is a division of Readerlink Distribution Services, LLC.
Silver Dolphin Books is a registered trademark of Readerlink Distribution Services, LLC.

The Smithsonian name and logo are registered trademarks of the Smithsonian Institution.
All notations of errors or omissions should be addressed to Silver Dolphin Books, Editorial Department,
at the above address.

ISBN: 978-1-68412-320-9

Manufactured, printed, and assembled in Heshan, China. First printing, December 2017. HH/12/17.
21 20 19 18 17   1 2 3 4 5

Toy manufactured in Hong Kong.

Written by Emily Rose Oachs
Designed by Dynamo Limited

For Smithsonian Enterprises:
Kealy Gordon, Product Development Manager, Licensing
Ellen Nanney, Licensing Manager
Brigid Ferraro, Vice President, Education and Consumer Products
Carol LeBlanc, Senior Vice President, Education and Consumer Products
Chris Liedel, President

Image Credits:
Thinkstock, SuperStock, Inc., Nobu Tamura, Matteo De Stefano, NTNU Vitenskapsmuseet, Ghedoghedo,
Katsamenis, Martin R. Smith, Theodore W. Pietsch, SEFSC Pascagoula Laboratory; Collection of Brandi Noble,

Contents

Introduction to Oceans

Oceans cover more than two-thirds of the planet, and hold 97 percent of Earth's water. The oceans are important to life on Earth. There are five oceans on Earth: Pacific, Atlantic, Arctic, Indian, and (Antarctic) Southern oceans. They provide much-needed water and shape the **climate** and weather on Earth. And they are home to many of Earth's most amazing creatures!

OCEAN LIFE

Earth's oceans teem with life. More than 250,000 marine creatures have been identified so far! Kelp and seagrass grow from the ocean floor. Sharks, whales, and sea turtles swim through the open ocean. Bright fish hide among anemones and coral. An abundance of **plankton** also fills the ocean. Floating near the surface, plankton drifts through the oceans on currents. Plankton is made up of both animals, called zooplankton, and plants, called phytoplankton.

Plankton

The Water Cycle

The water cycle is how water moves around the planet. Most of Earth's rain starts in the oceans. The Sun's heat causes water from oceans and lakes to evaporate into water vapor. The vapor rises into Earth's atmosphere. As it rises, the vapor moves into cooler air and forms clouds. Eventually, the water vapor falls to Earth in the form of rain or snow. Back on Earth, it makes its way into oceans, rivers, and lakes. Then it happens all over again.

SALT IN THE SEA

Salt water fills the oceans. The salt actually comes from land! As rain falls, it picks up salt from rocks and soil and washes the salt into nearby rivers. Rivers then carry this salt to the ocean, where it builds up. There is a lot of salt in the oceans. Imagine if all of the oceans' salt were spread across Earth's land—it would stand 500 feet tall!

Journey into the Unknown

The oceans are a vast, largely unfamiliar frontier. Scientists believe that about 95 percent of the world's oceans remain unexplored. There are better maps of the planet Mars than there are of Earth's oceans! Each year, scientists find tens of thousands of new marine species. They believe that two-thirds of the oceans' animal species are just waiting to be discovered!

History of Oceans

**Oceans have had a long history on Earth.
They have washed over the planet for billions of years.**

The Origin of the Oceans

Early in Earth's history, erupting volcanoes released water vapor into Earth's atmosphere. The planet was so hot that the vapor remained as a gas. Eventually, the planet began to cool. The gas condensed into water, and rain began to fall. This rain fell for millions of years! It filled up the low-lying points on Earth's surface. These pools of water grew to become the oceans more than 4 billion years ago.

Some scientists believe that some of Earth's water also came from comets. Comets are frozen balls of ice and dirt that speed through space. Billions of years ago, comets crashed onto Earth's surface. They brought water from outer space to the planet. This water helped to fill Earth's oceans too!

THE FIRST LIFE

The oceans were likely the place where the first life **evolved** about 3.8 billion years ago. The first living creatures were not like the animals or plants that we see today. Rather, they were single-celled **organisms** called bacteria.

Bacteria

Over millions of years, single-celled organisms **evolved** and underwent tiny changes over a long period of time. Around 3.5 million years ago, organisms that were able to **photosynthesize** appeared. They fed on water, carbon dioxide, and sunlight to survive. It took more than a billion years for multicelled organisms to evolve. About 600 million years ago, animals came into being. That is three billion years after the first life on Earth appeared!

THE FIRST CONTINENTS

The planet and its oceans did not always look as they do today. At first, a single ocean likely covered the entire planet. Few islands dotted the water's surface. About 1 billion years ago, Rodinia was the sole continent on Earth. A single ocean, called Mirovia, surrounded it. But over hundreds of millions of years, the massive continent broke apart. The pieces spread around the planet, forming multiple smaller continents, causing new ocean channels to form. Earth's continents are always shifting very slowly. As they move, new oceans open up, while other oceans close. Over millions of years, this process has been repeated. The continents have combined into supercontinents and separated again several times.

CONTINENTAL DRIFT

BEFORE

AFTER

Prehistoric Treasures:
The First Fossils

Just as the first life evolved in the ocean, the earliest **fossils** are of marine organisms. Fossils of cyanobacteria found in the rocks of Australia are more than 3.5 billion years old. Cyanobacteria still exist today; they are tiny bacteria that live in water. They create their own energy through **photosynthesis**. Cyanobacteria use water, carbon dioxide, and sunlight to make their own food!

Ediacaran Fauna

About 600 million years ago, during the Ediacaran period, the continents held no life. But there was life along the floor of Earth's shallow seas. These organisms were relatively large, soft-bodied **invertebrates**. Some of them left behind traces of themselves.

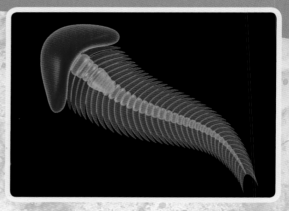

WHAT ARE FOSSILS?

Fossils are the preserved remains of long-dead plants, animals, or other creatures. From them, scientists learn about creatures that once existed. They learn what creatures roamed the planet and when, and help scientists piece together what the world once looked like.

In the 1940s, scientists discovered some of these trace fossils in Australia. They named them the Ediacaran fauna. These fossils were the first evidence of multicellular life in Earth's history. Previously, scientists had not found fossils of multicellular life any earlier than the Cambrian period, which began about 541 million years ago.

Some of the Ediacaran fauna looked like today's sea pens. Others looked similar to sea jellies. *Dickinsonia* was leaflike in shape and stretched almost five feet long!

Sea pen

TYPES OF FOSSILS

There are two types of fossils. Body fossils are the preserved remains of organisms that were once a part of an animal's body. Bones and teeth are examples of body fossils. Trace fossils are the preserved evidence of an organism. They show an organism's presence, movements, or behavior. Trace fossils may be an animal's footprint, the imprint of a leaf, or even dinosaur dung!

How Do Fossils Form?

It takes at least 10,000 years for a fossil to form. Shortly after death, an organism must quickly become buried by mud, sand, or other sediment. In time, the creature's soft parts usually decompose. But its hard parts, such as bones and teeth, remain. Over time, minerals from the sediment begin to replace the organism's bones. The weight of upper layers of sediment presses down. The pressure turns lower layers of the sediment into rock around the bone. And the minerals fully replace the bone so that all that is left are the fossilized remains of the organism.

Fossils, in general, rarely form. But when they do, they usually form on an organism's hard parts, such as a fish's bones or a shark's teeth. Fossils of soft-bodied organisms, such as jellyfish, are much rarer. Usually, the soft bodies decay before fossilization.

Prehistoric Treasures:
The Cambrian Explosion

Later, the Cambrian Explosion brought a burst of evolution. **Paleontologists** discovered a sudden diversity of life in marine fossils from around 541 million years ago. No longer did fossils show only traces of early soft-bodied multicellular organisms. Many fossils showed distinctive types of creatures that once called the oceans home.

Trilobites

Over a period of about 20 million years, the Cambrian Explosion produced early ancestors of creatures that still live today. The fossil record holds evidence of mollusks, corals, and sponges from the Cambrian period. With hard skeletons or shells, these creatures were more likely to fossilize than soft-bodied creatures of earlier periods.

TRILOBITES

Abundant in the fossil record are trilobites. These **extinct arthropods** dominated the seas of the Cambrian period. They lived from about 521 to 240 million years ago.

From fossils, paleontologists know that about 15,000 different species evolved before they became extinct. Each bore the same distinctive features of arthropods today. Among those were segmented bodies and exoskeletons that shed as they grew.

But there was a great diversity among the trilobites. Some, such as the *Acanthopleurella*, were a mere 0.04 inches long. Others, such as the *Isotelus rex*, grew to a massive 2.3 feet in length. Body shape varied immensely too. And although some trilobites boasted complex eyes with excellent vision, others were blind.

HALLUCIGENIA SPARSA

Hallucigenia fossils show an odd, wormlike creature. Two rows of spines adorned its back. On its belly, the *Hallucigenia's* clawed **tentacles** carried the creature across the seafloor.

Opabinia

Fossils of *Opabinia* show that this creature is unlike anything living today. With five eyes and a 1-inch-long flexible nose, the 3-inch *Opabinia* likely lived at the bottom of Cambrian seas. It possibly used its nose to dig into the seafloor sediment to capture worms!

HAPLOPHRENTIS CARINATUS

A coned shell protected the body of this small animal. Two arms kept the *Haplophrentis* stable in moving ocean waters. They may even have helped the creature swim and grab food!

Cambrian Predators

Tough **predators** during the Cambrian period were the *Anomalocaris canadensis*. The *Anomalocaris* were likely among the largest hunters at the time. Some grew to 3.3 feet long. Quick and deadly, they darted through the oceans as they hunted for trilobites. Swimming lobes propelled them through the oceans, while large, spiked front limbs reached out to grab **prey**. Their square mouths held strong teeth that crushed the shells of its arthropod prey!

Prehistoric Treasures:
Fish and Reptiles

Today, there are more than 24,000 species of fish on the planet. The first fish likely evolved about 468 million years ago, during the Ordovician Period. Later, the Devonian Period saw a huge diversification of fish. Many newly evolved fish, such as placoderms, appeared in the fossil record during this time, between about 418 and 354 million years ago. Sharks also trace their origin to this period.

Ichthyosaurs

Although marine **reptiles**, the bodies of ichthyosaurs were similar to today's dolphins. These ocean creatures were fierce predators. Most had large eyes, likely for spotting prey even in cloudy water. With long snouts, many ichthyosaurs had jaws that held sharp, cone-shaped teeth to help them catch prey, such as ammonites and belemnites. Although most averaged between 10 and 16 feet in length, some were the size of today's whales. The *Shonisaurus* was nearly 50 feet long!

THE ARMORED PLACODERMS

Huge fish known as placoderms called Earth's oceans home about 418 million years ago. Armor protected the heads and bodies of these predators. They died out by the end of the Devonian Period.

PLESIOSAURS

Long necks distinguished plesiosaurs from other marine reptiles. Fossils show that some plesiosaurs had 72 vertebrae! Yet not all plesiosaurs boasted this signature feature. Neck length varied greatly among the different plesiosaur species. Instead, some had short necks with lengthy skulls. Four flippers helped the plesiosaur navigate prehistoric oceans. Scientists believe the two front flippers propelled the plesiosaurs, while the two hind flippers steered.

When Reptiles Ruled the Seas

Just as **reptiles** known as dinosaurs came to rule the land, so too did marine reptiles dominate the seas. Starting around 252 million years ago, fierce marine reptiles began to appear. They swam the oceans through the Triassic, Jurassic, and Cretaceous periods. Yet all had disappeared by the mass extinction of the dinosaurs about 66 million years ago.

Mary Anning

Mary Anning was an avid nineteenth-century fossil collector. She grew up in a small town along England's Jurassic Coast.

As a child, Mary and her family collected **fossils** from the seashore near their home. They found many fascinating fossils of extinct marine creatures, such as ammonites and belemnites.

As a child, she and her brother together unearthed the first complete ichthyosaurus skeleton ever discovered! Later, Mary discovered the first-ever skeleton of the long-necked plesiosaur.

Mary's finds were not limited to marine creatures. She also found the skeleton of a pterosaur near her home. Later, she identified fossils that had long-stumped collectors—fossilized dung! Some call Mary "the greatest fossilist the world ever knew."

Fossils in the Backyard

Locked away in the world's rocks is evidence of life that lived long ago. Certain parts of the world are rich with fossils. Specific locations are known for the excellent fossils found there. Often, these fossils all come from a similar point in time. They stay hidden until someone starts to dig, unearthing the secrets of an Earth that existed millions of years ago.

A CHANGING PLANET

There is land that is dry today, but was once underwater. Scientists have found evidence of sea life in unexpected places. Shark fossils have been discovered in the foothills of the Italian Alps, while prehistoric marine predators have been dug up from the plains of Kansas. Scientists have even found whale fossils in the Andes Mountains!

Burgess Shale

Location: British Columbia, Canada
Time Period: Cambrian Period

A great deal of fossilized soft-bodied creatures have been found in the Burgess Shale. Scientists believe this is due to the environment. Hundreds of millions of years ago, underwater landslides buried unsuspecting organisms. This created conditions that allowed for the fossilization of even soft-bodied organisms. Paleontologists have recovered thousands of fossils from the Burgess Shale.

Niobrara Chalk Beds

Location: Kansas, United States
Time Period: Pennsylvanian, Permian, Cretaceous Periods

Shallow seas covered North America's Midwest about 130 million years ago. They divided the continent into two halves. During the Cretaceous Period, huge sea turtles, massive oysters, and fearsome fish swam over this land. Today, only their fossils remain, trapped in the limestone deposits and chalk beds of the Great Plains.

Jurassic Coast

Location: **England, United Kingdom**
Time Period: **Triassic, Jurassic, Cretaceous Periods**

Layers of sedimentary rock form cliffs that tower over the English Channel. For about 100 miles along the coast, these cliffs hold 185 million years of prehistory. As waves crash ashore, the water exposes the fossils of ancient marine creatures. During low tide, people can collect the fossils that have fallen from the cliffs. Hidden in these rocks are fossils of ancient marine reptiles, mollusks, fish, and even dinosaurs.

JURASSIC COAST FOSSIL : WIWAXIA

Fossils show Wiwaxia to be small, sluglike animals. They grew to about 2 inches, and had two rows of spines that ran the length of their backs. These likely offered the Wiwaxia some defense from predators.

JURASSIC COAST FOSSIL : AMMONITE

Related to today's nautilus, ammonites were prehistoric cephalopods with chambered, spiraled shells. Alive during the Jurassic and Cretaceous periods, ammonites evolved quickly. Because of this, paleontologists often use them to determine the ages of other nearby fossils. Usually only ammonite shells—but not their bodies—survive as fossils. They range in size from about the size of a thumbnail to about 8 feet across!

Today's Oceans

Today, five oceans cover the planet, and they are all connected. They are bordered by various gulfs and seas. And they separate the planet's seven continents.

Pacific Ocean

The Pacific Ocean is vast and deep. It is the world's largest ocean, covering almost one-third of the planet's surface. It has an area of more than 63,780,000 square miles. The Pacific Ocean takes up more space than all of Earth's continents combined!

Atlantic Ocean

Although the second-largest ocean, the Atlantic is about half the size of the Pacific Ocean. The Atlantic is the youngest ocean on Earth, formed just 1.8 million years ago. It separates Europe and Africa in the east from North America and South America in the west.

MID-OCEANIC RIDGE

The Atlantic Ocean's waves hide an underwater mountain range called the Mid-Atlantic Ridge. It follows the Atlantic Ocean's S-shape, carving down the ocean's center.

Southern Ocean

As the southernmost ocean, the Southern Ocean encircles Antarctica. It touches the Pacific Ocean, Atlantic Ocean, and Indian Ocean. The boundary where these oceans meet the Southern Ocean is called the Antarctic Convergence.

Arctic Ocean

Small and shallow, the Arctic Ocean sits at the top of the world. It covers and surrounds the North Pole. The ocean's waters are very cold. A thick layer of ice often covers much of the Arctic Ocean, especially in winter. In the summer, some of the ice melts. Land surrounds the Arctic Ocean on nearly all sides. Just a few seas and straits connect it to other oceans.

THE DEEPEST POINT

The Mariana Trench sits far below in the Pacific Ocean, and is the deepest point on Earth. Challenger Deep is 36,198 feet beneath the ocean's surface.

TSUNAMI DANGER

In 2004, a large, 9.1 earthquake struck about 100 miles off the coast of Sumatra, an Indonesian island in the Indian Ocean. This set off a powerful tsunami. Tsunamis are giant waves that occur when underwater earthquakes strike. They move quickly across the ocean. Sometimes they reach speeds of up to 500 miles per hour—the speed of a jet! In the Indian Ocean, the 2004 tsunami came with little warning. Walls of water up to 50 feet high washed ashore. It killed thousands of people and destroyed communities along the Indian Ocean's coast.

Indian Ocean

Africa, Australia, and Asia border the Indian Ocean on three sides. The Indian Ocean is the warmest ocean. Its warm waters appeal to humpback whales that **migrate** there to breed.

Underwater Landscapes

Many of the landscapes found on land also appear below the ocean's surface. Ocean waters hide meadows of seagrass and forests of kelp. Huge underwater mountain ranges stretch for thousands of miles, and volcanoes erupt from deep beneath the surface. Vast plains spread across the ocean floor, while valleys sink deep below the surface.

Mountain Ranges

Underwater mountain ranges, called the mid-ocean ridge, crisscross Earth's surface. They form along **tectonic plates**. Underwater volcanoes helped build these mountains.

Mid-ocean ridges trail through all of the oceans, stretching more than 46,000 miles. Their peaks stand thousands of feet above the ocean floor. In some cases, they even rise above the surface, forming islands such as Iceland.

Seafloor spreading occurs along these ridges. As the tectonic plates separate, **magma** seeps through the cracks in the crust and builds new ocean floor. In this way, new patches of Earth's crust are constantly being formed.

CONTINENTAL SHELF

The continental shelf extends out from the coasts. It is the edge of the continent, covered in waters up to 600 feet deep. As the sea level rises and falls, the width of the continental shelf grows and shrinks. The continental shelf angles gradually toward the open ocean. Eventually, it gives way to a steep slope that drops thousands of feet to the abyssal plain.

Iceland

THE RING OF FIRE

Most of Earth's volcanic activity takes place in ocean volcanoes. Much of this happens along the edges of the Pacific Ocean's Ring of Fire, an approximately 25,000-mile belt of volcanoes. More than 450 undersea volcanoes make up this chain. These volcanoes form at the edges of tectonic plates. When the plates meet, one is shoved below the other. Magma surges forth, forming volcanoes. A great deal of earthquake activity also occurs along the Ring of Fire.

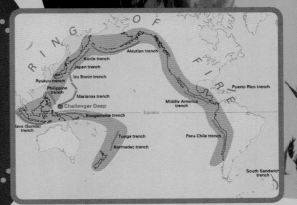

Abyssal Plain

Stretching wide across the deep ocean floor is the abyssal plain. This vast, flat area usually sits more than 14,500 feet below the ocean's surface.

Trenches

Steep valleys deep in the ocean are known as trenches. These trenches mark the limits of the ocean depths. The waters of the Pacific Ocean hide most major trenches, including the Mariana Trench. The Mariana Trench, the deepest, reaches nearly 7 miles below the surface.

UNDERWATER HOT SPRINGS

Deep underwater, hot springs form at cracks in the Earth's crust. Water seeps down into the cracks, where hot magma heats the water. The water rises back to the Earth's crust, spewing through vents in the ocean floor. Water erupting from these vents can reach temperatures of 700 degrees Fahrenheit!

Tides and Tide Pools

Tides bring the rise and fall of water along the ocean shore. They happen regularly, twice each day. They are caused by the Moon's gravity. The Moon's gravity tugs on the ocean water. It pulls the water in toward shore. This is high tide. Later, it pulls the water back out to sea. This is low tide. Whether it is high or low tide depends on the Moon's position relative to Earth.

The Intertidal Zone

The land where shore meets sea is called the intertidal zone. This is the part of the shore that is underwater during high tide, but exposed during low tide. Five main regions make up the intertidal zone:

1. Splash:

The splash zone is mostly dry. Usually, water only reaches the splash zone from the mist and spray of the crashing waves. Little sea life is found in the splash zone. Those creatures that do live there are able to survive being out of the water and in the open air for long periods.

Splash Zone inhabitants:
periwinkles, small barnacles

2. High:

Water floods the high zone only during the highest tides. Animals here spend most of their time in the open air.

High Zone inhabitants:
limpets, periwinkles

TIDE POOLS

When high tide flows in, water floods the shore. But when high tide retreats, not all of the sea water returns to the ocean with it. Instead, some water remains trapped among the shore's rocks in shallow pools. These shallow pools of sea water are called tide pools. They appear only twice each day, during low tide. And they teem with colorful, diverse sea life.

3. Middle:

During high tide, the middle zone is underwater. Low tide sees the middle zone exposed to the open air. Animals here spend about half of each day underwater and half of each day exposed.

Middle Zone inhabitants: sea lettuce, hermit crabs

4. Low:

Usually, the low zone is submerged. Only the lowest tides of the year reveal this zone.

Low Zone inhabitants: nudibranchs, sea urchins, blue-ringed octopus

5. Subtidal:

Below the other zones is the subtidal zone. It sits just beyond the point of low tide. This area is always underwater. Some creatures move freely between the subtidal zone and the other intertidal zones.

Subtidal Zone inhabitants: fish, sea stars, sea urchins

Animals
of the Tide Pools

Each day sees the rise and fall of the tides. The plants and animals of the intertidal zone must be tough organisms. Twice each day, they are completely underwater. And twice each day, they are fully exposed to open air and sunlight. Creatures of the tide pools have adapted to survive this constant state of change.

Common Periwinkle

Size: up to 1.5 inches

Diet: algae

Range: Atlantic Ocean

Like other snails, periwinkles use their flat, muscular foot to move around. The foot helps periwinkles survive in tide pools. It allows them to tightly grip the sides of rocks. This prevents periwinkles from being washed away in strong waves!

Tidepool Sculpin

Size: up to 3.5 inches long

Diet: worms, crustaceans

Range: Pacific Ocean

Sometimes, high tide goes out and leaves these tiny fish high and dry. They have no way to return to the water. But a special adaptation helps these small fish survive such situations. Their gills allow them to breathe underwater. But the tidepool sculpin is also able to breathe air directly! This allows them to survive until high tide flows in again.

ABOUT SEA STARS

Tiny suction-cup feet line the underside of a sea star's body. They allow the sea star to creep across the ocean floor and cling to the sides of rocks. Sea stars love to eat mussels, clams, and other mollusks. When it comes time to feed, a sea star uses its tube feet to pry the shells of its prey apart. Then, it ejects its stomach through its mouth. The stomach digests the meat and then returns to the sea star's body.

LITTLE STINGERS

Strong suction feet keep aggregating anemones firmly attached to rocks. The anemones do not move. But they are still able to hunt and protect themselves. Their tentacles have stinging cells called **nematocysts**. These keep many predators away. And moving water carries tiny animals past aggregating anemones. The anemone's tentacles sting and stun the animals. Then, the anemone eats the prey.

TIDE-POOL PROTECTION

When low tide comes, the sea star is vulnerable to attacks from seagulls and other shore birds. But even if the sea star loses an arm, the creature is able to re-grow it!

Ochre Sea Stars

Size: up to 18 inches across

Diet: mussels, barnacles, snails

Range: Pacific Ocean

Ochre sea stars are brightly colored creatures. They may be purple, orange, or brown. These sea stars are key predators of mussels. By eating many mussels, ochre sea stars keep mussel populations in check. Otherwise, mussels would reproduce quickly, spreading across the rocks. There would be little room left for other species to live and grow in the intertidal zone.

Aggregating Sea Anemones

Size: up to 3.5 inches

Diet: small fish, snails

Range: Pacific Ocean

Large, dense colonies of aggregating anemones live in tide pools. When underwater, an anemone's tentacles spread out like flower petals around its central mouth. But when water retreats, the anemone pulls its tentacles in tight. Bits of sand, rock, and shells cling to its body. These help keep the anemone from drying out until high tide returns.

Animals
of the Tide Pools

The Highest High Tide

In some parts of the world, there is little difference between high and low tides. But in other parts of the world, the difference is much more pronounced. Canada's Bay of Fundy claims the highest high tides. At certain times of the year, there may be a 53-foot difference between highest point of high tide and the lowest point of low tide!

ODD HOMES

As garbage fills the oceans, hermit crabs have started to find unusual, manmade places to call home. Now, they are not limited solely to items from the natural world. Hermit crabs have been spotted sporting homes made out of bottle caps, broken glass bottles, and even Legos.

Black Oystercatcher

Size: up to 19 inches long

Diet: mussels, whelks, limpets

Range: Pacific Ocean

Black oystercatchers plan their days around the tides. The birds usually rest during high tide, but when the tide goes out, they start moving toward the shore. The retreating tide exposes some of their favorite foods! The black oystercatcher has a long, strong bill. The bill's shape and strength are ideal for prying mussels and other shellfish from rocks. The bird pokes its sharp bill into partially opened mussel shells, then rips the meat out.

Hermit Crab

Size: up to about 3 inches

Diet: plants, small pieces of dead animals

Range: Atlantic Ocean, Indian Ocean, Pacific Ocean

Unlike other crustaceans, hermit crabs do not grow their own shells. Rather, they move into empty periwinkle or whelk shells. As a hermit crab grows, it abandons its shell for a larger one. That way, the hermit crab makes sure its soft, curved body is always protected from predators. Hermit crabs are found on ocean shores around the world.

Important to the nudibranch's diet are creatures called hydroids. Hydroids have stinging cells known as nematocysts. When the nudibranch eats hydroids, the nematocysts run through its system. They are stored in the nudibranch's cerata. Then, when predators try to eat the nudibranch, they get a nasty sting!

Blue-Ringed Octopus

Size: up to 8 inches long

Diet: crabs, mollusks, small fish

Range: Indian Ocean, Pacific Ocean

Found along Australia's coasts, the blue-ringed octopus hides among the rocks of tide pools. It is a dangerous tide pool creature. Its venom is strong enough to kill a person! The cephalopod's name comes from its coloration. When alarmed, the 60 blue rings that dot its skin start to brighten. This is a warning to stay away!

Opalescent Nudibranch

Size: up to 3.14 inches long

Diet: hydroids, sea pens, small sea anemones

Range: Pacific Ocean

The opalescent nudibranch is a small, brightly-colored creature. An orange stripe runs down its back, while two blue stripes run along its sides. On the opalescent nudibranch's back are fringed, fingerlike structures called cerata. The nudibranch absorbs oxygen through its skin. More cerata give it more places to take in oxygen!

The Rocky Coasts

Many marine animals live on and near the oceans' rocky shores. The rocky shores can be an unforgiving environment. Waves crash against the rocks. The twice-daily rise and fall of the tides means the **habitat** is always changing.

SUSPENSION FEEDING

Acorn barnacles are **suspension feeders**. They filter food out of the water that flows over them. When underwater, acorn barnacles open their shells. Tiny fringed feet, called cirri, extend into the water. The cirri catch food, such as tiny plankton, that float past!

For some creatures, the rocky shore is a brief refuge. It offers a chance to rest in the warm sun. For other creatures, the rocky shore is a permanent home. They latch on and never move. Still other creatures seek shelter in the lush seabeds that lay just beyond the rocky coasts.

Underwater, these shallow rocky shores create a rich habitat. Cliffs provide a safe, stable home for jewel anemones. Lobsters make their homes in the irregularities of the rock. Some small fish find protection among the seaweed, while other fish search along the rocky coasts for prey.

Stonefish

Size: up to 16 inches

Diet: crustaceans, fish

Range: Indian Ocean, Pacific Ocean

The stonefish can be hard to spot on rocky ocean floors near Australia. With bumpy skin and varied coloring, the stonefish's **camouflage** helps it ambush prey and keep predators away. But even if a predator attacks, the stonefish is well-armed. A row of sharp, venom-filled spines trail down its back. When threatened, the stonefish raises the spines. Then, the fish can inject the dangerous venom into its attackers. No other fish in the world is as venomous!

Acorn Barnacle

Size: up to 4 inches across

Diet: plankton

Range: Atlantic Ocean, Pacific Ocean

Acorn barnacles produce a strong glue to attach themselves to hard surfaces. But they do not always live such immobile lives. Young acorn barnacles start life as larvae. They float freely through the ocean for the first few weeks of life. Eventually, they settle and fasten themselves to a rock.

Leafy Sea Dragon

Size: up to 16 inches long

Diet: krill, shrimp, plankton

Range: Indian Ocean

Just off of the rocky shores of southern and western Australia, hidden among the seaweed, is the leafy sea dragon. These fish are rare, but they are also hard to spot. Long, frilly appendages grow from the leafy sea dragon's body. These appendages look like leaves! They help the fish blend in with the seaweed. Leafy sea dragons are slow-moving fish. Their appendages wave in the water. This makes them look even more like seaweed, and helps them camouflage from predators.

Animals
of the Rocky Coasts

Many types of seals and sea lions enjoy rocky shores. Both animals hoist themselves out of the water to lay on the rocks. This is known as "hauling out." Seals and sea lions haul out in groups called rookeries where they bask in the sun. They socialize with other members of their rookeries, but they head to the water again when it is time to hunt.

Sea Lion vs. Seal

Despite their similarities, there are key differences between seals and sea lions.

Flippers

Movement on land is more awkward for a seal than a sea lion. A seal's fur-covered front flippers are shorter than the skin-covered flippers of a sea lion, making movement more difficult. And unlike seals, sea lions are able to rotate their hind flippers. They can position them under their bodies. This allows them to use all four limbs to walk on land. Seals, instead, must bounce on their bellies to move.

Ears

Sea lions have small but visible flaps that cover their ears. But seals are often called "earless." They have ears, but they are difficult to see. Only from up close are a seal's earholes visible.

Sound

Both seals and sea lions make sounds, but sea lions are much noisier. They release loud, sharp barks into the air. Seals, on the other hand, are quieter. They usually grunt and groan.

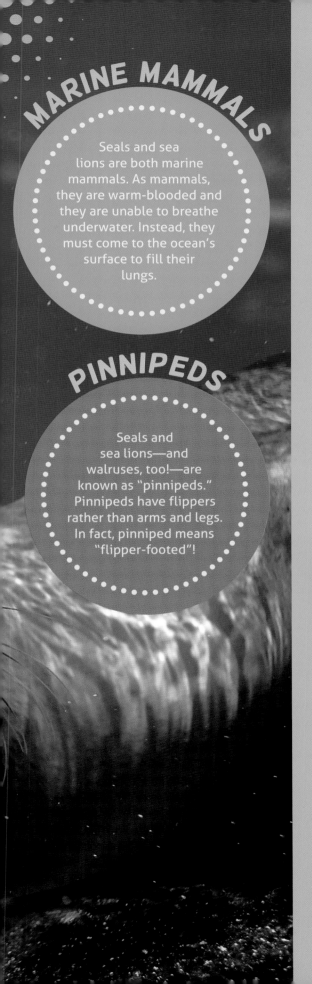

MARINE MAMMALS

Seals and sea lions are both marine mammals. As mammals, they are warm-blooded and they are unable to breathe underwater. Instead, they must come to the ocean's surface to fill their lungs.

PINNIPEDS

Seals and sea lions—and walruses, too!—are known as "pinnipeds." Pinnipeds have flippers rather than arms and legs. In fact, pinniped means "flipper-footed"!

California Sea Lion

Length: up to 7.25 feet

Weight: up to 860 pounds

Diet: fish, squid

Range: Pacific Ocean

California sea lions hunt in the open ocean. They may dive as deep as 656 feet to dine on fish, squid, and other prey. They can remain underwater for up to 10 minutes! But these marine mammals are also common sights on rocky coasts. Several thousand sea lions may gather on the rocks. It is on rocky coasts that they also breed and give birth.

Harbor Seal

Length: up to 5 feet

Weight: up to 245 pounds

Diet: fish, squid, crabs

Range: Atlantic Ocean, Pacific Ocean

Harbor seals spend much of their time on land. Even on land, they are round, awkward looking creatures. They move by crawling on their bellies. But in the water, harbor seals are far more agile. They can swim fast and far, and dive deep in search of food. Harbor seals come to rocky shores in small rookeries.

The Coral Reef

Corals are tiny, soft-bodied polyps. They live close to other coral polyps in large groups called colonies. Although each coral polyp is small, colonies can reach the size of cars! One end of the coral polyp attaches to a hard surface, such as rock or the skeletons of other corals. The polyp's mouth stands at the other end. Stinging tentacles surround it. These tentacles keep predators away. They also help polyps collect passing zooplankton to eat.

Building Reefs

Coral reefs are built of stony corals. When stony corals die, they leave behind their hard skeletons. Other coral polyps anchor themselves to those remains. When those corals die, others attach to the remaining skeletons. The cycle continues. Over time, coral skeletons build up into large structures and form coral reefs. Coral reefs grow slowly. Most corals only grow 1 inch each year at most. It can take thousands of years for a coral reef to form.

CORAL TYPES

Some corals are soft corals, such as whip coral and sea fans. They are made of more flexible material that sways in the moving water. Other corals are stony corals, such as brain coral and elkhorn coral. These build hard, mineral skeletons around themselves.

ZOOXANTHELLAE

The bright colors of coral come from tiny organisms called zooxanthellae. Zooxanthellae are algae that live in the tissues of many corals in shallow, tropical waters. Both organisms benefit from this. The coral protects the zooxanthellae. It also provides the algae with key nutrients. During photosynthesis, the zooxanthellae produces food that gets passed to the coral. This food is necessary for the coral to grow. The coral needs the zooxanthellae to survive!

Pygmy Seahorse

Size: up to 1 inch long

Diet: plankton

Range: Pacific Ocean

Pygmy seahorses are well-equipped for survival in Australia's coral reefs. Their skin matches the color and texture of a sea fan. This camouflages these tiny animals against the coral. Pygmy seahorses wrap their tails around the sea fan. This keeps them from drifting away.

Clown Anemonefish

Size: up to 4 inches

Diet: algae

Range: Indian Ocean, Pacific Ocean

Clown anemonefish make their homes in the stinging tentacles of sea anemones. A mucus coating protects the fish from the anemone's stings. But predators, afraid of being stung themselves, stay away. The anemone's tentacles keep the clown anemonefish safe.

Hidden in Plain Sight

Scientists first discovered pygmy seahorses in 1970. They had brought sea fans into their lab to study. Only then did they notice the well-hidden hitchhikers on the coral!

MUTUALISM

Sea anemones benefit from having clown anemonefish around, too. While the anemones keep the anemonefish safe, the anemonefish keeps its host clean. It eats parasites that live among the anemones tentacles!

Animals
of the Coral Reef

From sharks and eels to parrotfish and sea anemones, colorful coral reefs are home to a great diversity of ocean life. Nooks and crannies in the reef provide secure shelter for many creatures. Food for both carnivores and herbivores is also abundant there. Coral reefs take up less than 1 percent of the ocean. Yet scientists estimate that 25 percent of all ocean species call coral reefs home.

Spotted Eagle Ray

Width: up to 10 feet

Weight: up to 500 pounds

Diet: mollusks, fish, cephalopods, crustaceans

Range: Atlantic Ocean, Indian Ocean, Pacific Ocean

Spotted eagle rays often head into coral reefs to feed. There, they hunt for fish, giant clams, and other prey along the seafloor. In the open ocean, hundreds of spotted eagle rays may join together in a school. They appear to move gracefully through the water. Their wide, wing-like fins move up and down—appearing to flap—as they travel through the ocean. Spotted eagle rays are so powerful that they can leap out of the water!

Whitetip Reef Shark

Length: up to 6.5 feet

Weight: up to 37 pounds

Diet: fish, octopus, lobsters, crab

Range: Indian Ocean, Pacific Ocean

White spots on the tips of this shark's fins earned this shark its name. Whitetip reef sharks are nocturnal animals. Usually active at night, they take shelter with other whitetip reef sharks during the day. At night, they search the crevices of the coral reef for octopuses, fish, and other prey. Sometimes, they slam into coral as they hunt for prey. Tough skin protects them from the coral's sharp edges.

A SLEEPING COCOON

Each night, a queen parrotfish spins itself a thin cocoon made of mucus. This light covering provides protection from predators because it hides the parrotfish's scent!

ABOUT JELLYFISH

Jellyfish are about 95 percent water! They have no brains, hearts, or bones. Their transparent, circular bodies are called bells. Tentacles hang down from the bell, ready to capture prey and sting predators.

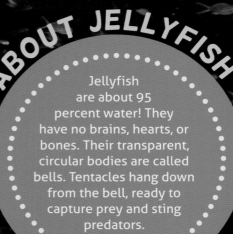

Queen Parrotfish

Size: up to 24 inches long

Diet: algae

Range: Atlantic Ocean

Parrotfish are brightly-colored fish of the coral reef. Their beaklike mouths hold strong teeth that help parrotfish scrape algae from rocks. Parrotfish also crunch coral to eat the algae that covers it. Their teeth are able to grind the coral into sand, which is released back into the ocean!

Box Jellyfish

Width: 12 inches

Length: 10 feet

Diet: shrimp, small fish

Range: Indian Ocean, Pacific Ocean

No other animal in the ocean is as venomous as the box jellyfish. Its deadly sting, delivered through its tentacles, can kill a human in minutes. With colorless cube-shaped bells, these creatures are tough to spot in the warm tropical waters they live in. And their many long tentacles make them even more dangerous.

The Great Barrier Reef

Stretching along Australia's northeastern coast is the Great Barrier Reef. Extending for 1,600 miles this is the world's largest coral reef! More than 400 species of coral make up this massive reef, providing homes to more than 1,500 types of fish. It first began to form more than 20,000 years ago!

Peacock Mantis Shrimp

Length: up to 6 inches long

Diet: gastropods, crabs, fish

Range: Indian Ocean, Pacific Ocean

The peacock mantis shrimp is a powerful and aggressive predator. With its exceptional eyesight, it waits for prey, such as crabs or fish, to come close. When prey nears, the peacock mantis shrimp unleashes the power of its clublike arms. They can strike prey at a speed of 75 miles per hour! This strength allows the brightly colored shrimp to prey on animals larger than itself. It can also shatter the shells of crabs and snails.

Giant Clam

Width: up to 4 feet

Weight: up to 500 pounds

Diet: zooplankton, nutrients from zooxanthellae

Range: Pacific Ocean, Indian Ocean

Giant clams are the world's largest bivalves! They are suspension feeders, but giant clams also get energy from the zooxanthellae that live inside their tissues. The zooxanthellae enjoy a safe home, while giant clams receive important nutrients from the algae. Giant clams would not survive without the zooxanthellae's help! Adult giant clams are anchored to the ocean floor. They spread their shells wide to catch the sun's rays during the day.

LOCATION

Corals appear throughout the ocean. They grow in the dark ocean depths. They also thrive in shallow waters. Coral reefs mostly form in warmer tropical or subtropical waters.

PREHISTORIC TREASURES: INOCERAMUS

Cretaceous seas that covered present-day Kansas were once home to colonies of the *Inoceramus*. This massive prehistoric clam stretched 6 feet across! Paleontologists have discovered fish fossils with *Inoceramus* fossils. They believe that fish sought shelter within the *Inoceramus's* shells!

Porcupinefish

Size: up to 35 inches long

Diet: snails, sea urchins, hermit crabs

Range: Atlantic Ocean, Indian Ocean, Pacific Ocean

A unique adaptation keeps porcupinefish safe from predators. When threatened, a porcupinefish quickly gulps in water. This inflates its body into a ball shape. It can balloon up to three times its normal size! Spines that usually lay flat against its skin stand upright.

Lionfish

Length: up to 11.8 inches long

Diet: crabs, shrimp, fish

Range: Western Pacific Ocean, Eastern Indian Ocean, Atlantic Ocean

Red stripes adorn the bodies of lionfish and their showy, fanlike fins. The lionfish spreads its fins wide to herd and trap prey against rocks and reefs. Lionfish may be easy to spot, but they have little to fear from predators. Venom fills the spines along their backs. If predators attack, they will receive a nasty sting!

Kelp Forests

Hidden beneath the ocean waves are tall underwater forests made of kelp, or seaweed. In some parts of the ocean, these tangled forests of brown seaweed rise up from the ocean floor. They form a broad, thick canopy at the ocean's surface.

Kelp may stand 100 feet tall, reaching from the ocean floor to its surface. These forests are also fast growing. One kelp plant may grow 20 inches in a single day!

Kelp forests thrive in shallow, temperate waters. Strong roots called holdfasts secure them to the rocky bottom. Kelp plants rely on sunlight for photosynthesis. Without sunlight, they cannot grow. So, unless the water is very clear, most kelp forests do not grow in ocean water deeper than 131 feet.

FLOATING TO THE SUN

Some types of kelp grow small gas-filled sacs on their stipes, or stalks. These sacs are called floats. They provide buoyancy to the stipes. Instead of the stipes sinking into the water, the floats help them rise toward the surface. That way, the kelp can get as much sunlight as it needs to grow.

Leopard Shark

Length: up to 6 feet
Weight: up to 50 pounds
Diet: crabs, fish, clams
Range: Pacific Ocean

Distinctive dark spots dot the body of a leopard shark, just like its land-bound namesake. These sharks prefer shallow waters. They often join many other leopard sharks to form large schools. Leopard sharks spend most of their days swimming along the ocean floor and through kelp forests. A leopard shark's mouth is located on the underside of its flat head. This makes it easy for the shark to pick up prey, such as crabs and rockfish, from the seafloor as it swims past.

Spiny Brittle Star

Size: up to 11.8 inches across
Diet: tiny plant particles
Range: Pacific Ocean

Spiny brittle stars are a common sight in kelp forests near California's coast. Millions of them may group together. They can form a thick coating on the seafloor! Often, spiny brittle stars hide themselves out of sight. They may tuck themselves under rocks or cover themselves with sand. This keeps them safe from predators. But spiny brittle stars are suspension feeders. So, they allow two or three of their arms to remain visible. Their tube feet collect tiny particles of food that drift past.

Animals
of the Kelp Forest

Underwater kelp forests bear some similarities to land forests. Diverse plants and animals call them home. And both offer food and shelter to their inhabitants.

Forest Maintenance

Sea otters are important for maintaining the health of kelp forests. They are a primary predator of sea urchins, which eat kelp. By hunting the sea urchins, the sea otters keep the sea urchin populations in check.

Without sea otters, sea urchin populations could grow too large. Vast numbers of sea urchins could destroy a kelp forest simply by feeding themselves. This would leave the diverse plants and animals that live in kelp forests without a home.

RESTING IN THE KELP

When it comes time to rest, sea otters wrap kelp around themselves to stay in place. Sometimes, they hold the paw of a neighboring sea otter. That way, they do not float away while they sleep!

Sea Otter

Length: up to 4.4 feet

Weight: up to 92 pounds

Diet: sea urchins, clams, mussels, squid, abalones

Range: Pacific Ocean

Sea otters are among the few types of mammals that use tools. Sometimes, they bring rocks along while hunting. The rocks help them to pry prey from underwater surfaces. Other times, sea otters use them after hunting. Back at the ocean's surface, they float on their backs with their collected mollusks on their bellies. The sea otters use the rocks to crack open mollusk shells. Then, they eat the meat inside!

Red Abalone

Size: up to 11.8 inches across

Diet: kelp, algae

Range: Pacific Ocean

Red abalones are the largest type of abalone. Three or four holes line the edge of an abalone's shell. The abalone uses these holes to breathe. Red abalones often seek shelter in deep cracks on the rocky ocean floor to avoid sea otters and other predators.

Purple Sea Urchin

Size: up to 4 inches across

Diet: algae

Range: Pacific Ocean

Moveable spines up to 3 inches long cover the hard body of a purple sea urchin. The spines grow from the sea urchin's test, a round, hard interior shell. Among the spines are tube feet that help the sea urchin move around. The purple sea urchin's mouth is on its underside. Hard, toothlike structures help the sea urchin scrape algae from rocks.

Icy Waters

The Arctic Ocean and Southern Ocean are the northernmost and southernmost oceans, respectively. Ice covers much of the Arctic Ocean throughout the year, while the waters of the Southern Ocean are similarly frigid. Yet life is able to thrive in these extreme habitats. Certain adaptations help animals of the Arctic and Southern Oceans survive.

A Colder Freeze

Usually, water freezes at 32 degrees Fahrenheit. But the salt in seawater causes oceans to freeze at the even lower 30 degrees Fahrenheit!

In 2017, a large crack broadened across one of Antarctica's ice shelves. As a result, a giant piece of ice broke away from the ice shelf. It was adrift in the ocean. The iceberg was approximately the size of the U.S. state of Delaware!

ICEBERGS

Icebergs originate from ice shelves or glaciers on land. They form when large ice chunks break away, or calve, from the edge of the glacier or ice shelf. Once in the water, the ice chunks are called icebergs. Icebergs may be the size of cars or even larger. Currents move them around the ocean. Scientists estimate that as many as 50,000 icebergs calve from Greenland glaciers each year!

Ice Movers

Penguins were designed for life in the water. They are excellent, graceful swimmers. Their wings act as flippers as they dive deep into the ocean to hunt for krill and fish. On land, these birds waddle awkwardly. Sometimes, they slide on their bellies across the ice!

Emperor Penguin

Height: up to 45 inches

Weight: up to 100 pounds

Diet: fish, krill, squid

Range: Antarctica/Southern Ocean

Vast crowds of penguins come together to form groups called rookeries. In these, penguins huddle together. Huddling keeps them warm against the wind, snow, and icy cold of Antarctica. Winter temperatures can drop as low as -40 degrees Fahrenheit! During breeding season, the female lays the egg, leaving the male to incubate it while she hunts. The male balances the egg on the tops of his feet for two months until it hatches.

Two coats of fur keep polar bears warm. The shaggier outer coat is made up of clear, hollow hairs. These give the bear its white appearance. A shorter, denser coat rests beneath. This wooly fur provides the bear further insulation in the cold and the icy waters.

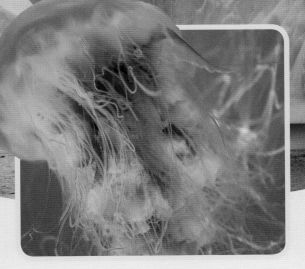

Lion's Mane Jellyfish

Width: 6 feet across

Length: up to 49 feet long

Diet: zooplankton, small fish

Range: Arctic Ocean, Northern Atlantic Ocean, Northern Pacific Ocean

No other jellyfish is larger than the lion's mane. A lion's mane jellyfish with stinging tentacles 120 feet long has been documented!

Polar Bear

Length: up to 8.5 feet

Weight: up to 1,320 pounds

Diet: seals, whales, walruses

Range: Arctic Ocean

Polar bears are strong swimmers. They may swim 60 miles or more as they search for food! In the winter, breathing holes help them hunt. There, polar bears patiently wait for seals to come to the surface to breathe. With its clawed paw, the polar bear grabs the seal and eats it!

Animals
of the Icy Waters

Marine mammals are warm-blooded creatures. Yet many—such as walruses, whales, seals, and sea lions—make icy ocean waters their homes. These marine mammals depend on blubber to stay warm. Blubber is a thick layer of fat below the skin. It insulates the mammal's body against the icy waters. It keeps them from losing too much body heat.

Narwhal

Length: up to 20 feet

Weight: up to 3,500 pounds

Diet: shrimp, squid, fish

Range: Arctic Ocean, Northern Atlantic Ocean

Breathing Holes

Breathing holes in the ice are important for marine mammals in cold regions. Mammals are unable to breathe underwater. They must come up for air. So, they keep ice holes open for breathing. Walruses use their tusks to create breathing holes. They wield their tusks as a chisel to keep holes clear of ice!

Weddell seals start on their holes when the ice is still thin. They use their teeth to carve openings into the thin ice. They continue to work to keep the hole open

Narwhals are toothed whales. But for males, one of their teeth takes on a unique pattern—it grows directly out of their heads. The tooth forms a spiraled, pointed tusk that can reach lengths of 8 feet or more! Some, but few, females also have tusks. Scientists believe these tusks have a variety of uses. Some have seen narwhals slap at fish with their tusks. This stuns the fish, allowing narwhals to eat them. Long tusks also help males impress females, and males can use them to fight

A USEFUL MUSTACHE

Walruses dive for food in shallow water where they hunt along the seafloor. Whiskers around their mouths help them detect clams, snails, and other food.

Weddell Seal

Length: up to 11 feet

Weight: up to 1,100 pounds

Diet: ice fish, crustaceans, cephalopods, cod

Range: Southern Ocean

Weddell seals are only found in the waters surrounding Antarctica. No other type of marine mammal lives as far south! Weddell seals are deep divers. They may swim as deep as 1,970 feet below the ocean's surface. Like other mammals, they need to breathe at the surface. Still, these seals have great lung capacity. They can stay underwater 80 minutes or more!

Walrus

Length: up to 11.5 feet

Weight: up to 3,000 pounds

Diet: mollusks, snails, crabs

Range: Arctic Ocean, Northern Atlantic Ocean, Northern Pacific Ocean

A walrus's tusks make this pinniped easy to identify. Tusks appear on both males and females, but they grow largest in males. Sometimes, the tusks grow to more than 3 feet in length and can weigh up to 12 pounds! Walruses love to socialize with other walruses. They are usually found in groups, both in the sea and when they haul out onto the ice.

Open Ocean

Out in the open ocean, water stretches to the horizon. The coasts are far away. The ocean floor may lie hundreds or even thousands of feet below the surface. It is impossible to be alone in the ocean because creatures live in every part of it. They fill each of the ocean's layers, from the ocean's surface to its deepest depths, from the coast of one continent to another.

Moon Jellyfish

Size: up to 12 inches across

Diet: plankton

Range: Atlantic Ocean, Indian Ocean, Pacific Ocean

Moon jellyfish are found around the world. Short, fringelike tentacles encircle the bell. The tentacles draw food toward the moon jellyfish's mouth, which is located on the underside of its bell. Moon jellyfish are slow swimmers. They propel themselves through the open ocean by pulsating their bells. By pulling water into the bell and then pushing it out again, the jellyfish moves forward.

PREHISTORIC TREASURES: ARCHELON

In 1896, paleontologists digging in South Dakota rocks unearthed the fossilized skeleton of a giant, extinct sea turtle. They estimated the *Archelon ischyros* had lived during the Cretaceous period, more than 100 million years ago. It made its home in the shallow, prehistoric seas that once covered today's Kansas. More discoveries of Archelon ischyros skeletons revealed it was far bigger than the leatherback, the largest of today's sea turtles. The Archelon likely weighed nearly 5,000 pounds. From tip to tail, the largest measured 13 feet long. From flipper to flipper, it was 16 feet across!

AN ANCIENT FAMILY

Scientists can trace the origins of jellyfish back millions of years. They believe that the first ancestors of today's jellyfish lived as long as 700 million years ago. This makes jellyfish hundreds of millions of years older than the dinosaurs!

Green Sea Turtle

Length: up to 3.5 feet

Weight: up to 400 pounds

Diet: sea grass, algae

Range: Atlantic Ocean, Indian Ocean, Pacific Ocean

The life of a young green sea turtle begins on land. It hatches from a nest on a sandy beach. Immediately after hatching, the sea turtle makes its way to the ocean. Once in the ocean, scientists believe they ride the currents through the open ocean for years. As adults, green sea turtles may spend time along coasts. But they set out on long migrations through the open ocean to breed. Some may travel more than 600 miles!

Leatherback Sea Turtle

Length: up to 7 feet

Weight: up to 2,000 pounds

Diet: jellyfish

Range: Atlantic Ocean, Indian Ocean, Pacific Ocean

The shells of leatherback sea turtles are not made up of hard plates. Instead, they are made up of a flexible, leathery material, which is what gives the turtles their name. Leatherback sea turtles are the largest turtles in the world. They are well-known for their lengthy migrations between their feeding and breeding grounds. Scientists recorded the migration of one leatherback sea turtle that was 13,000 miles long!

Animals
of the Open Ocean

Zones of the Open Ocean

Scientists divide the open ocean into different zones. Throughout the day, ocean creatures may move between the zones. They may undertake daily migrations to feed in one but sleep in another.

Closest to the surface is the sunlit zone. It stretches just 660 feet below the surface. Most ocean life calls this zone home.

SCHOOLING

Various types of fish, such as tuna and anchovies, swim through the ocean in huge groups called schools. Schooling may provide these groups safety from predators. Maintaining a specific distance from their neighbors, schooling fish are able to move through the ocean as if they are one animal. Predators may mistake the school of many smaller fish for a single large fish. Or, the school's constant, coordinated change in direction may confuse the predator!

Below, the twilight zone stretches to 3,300 feet below the ocean's surface. Little light reaches the twilight zone. Plants are unable to survive there, and some animals have transparent bodies, making them difficult to spot in the semi-darkness.

All water deeper than 3,300 feet is the deep ocean. The deep ocean makes up more than 75 percent of the ocean. There, the water is frigid and pure darkness. No light can penetrate to these depths. Still, animals thrive in this cold, dark place.

Krill

Size: up to 2 inches long

Diet: phytoplankton, algae

Range: Arctic Ocean, Atlantic Ocean, Indian Ocean, Pacific Ocean, Southern Ocean

Despite their tiny size, shrimplike krill are very important animals in the ocean. They are key players in the food chain. From whales to penguins, seals to squid, many ocean animals prey upon these small creatures. Vast swarms of krill—many yards wide and deep—gather at the ocean's surface. Predators swim through, gulping up hundreds of these small creatures at a time.

Pacific Sardines

Size: up to 16 inches

Diet: zooplankton

Range: Atlantic Ocean, Indian Ocean, Pacific Ocean

Pacific sardines can form massive schools that contain millions! The fish swim in coordinated movements. Schools offer the fish protection from predators. Many types of animals feed on sardines. Each spring, sardines head to more northern waters to breed. When autumn comes, they migrate back south.

Sailfish

Length: up to 11 feet

Weight: up to 220 pounds

Diet: sardines, anchovies

Range: Atlantic Ocean, Indian Ocean, Pacific Ocean

A large, sail-like dorsal fin gives the sailfish its name. Up to 30 sailfish work together to hunt large schools of sardines and other small fish in the open ocean. One sailfish will leap out of the water near the school. It corrals the school into a large ball of frantic fish. Other sailfish then dart in. They sweep their long, spearlike bills through the mass of fish, stunning fish that they then eat.

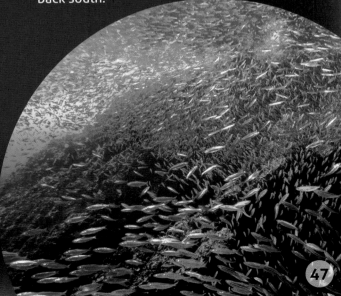

Cephalopods
of the Open Ocean

Cephalopods include octopuses, squids, nautiluses, and cuttlefish. They are types of mollusks. Appropriately, their name means "head foot." Their legs are attached directly to their heads, radiating outward. Cephalopods are quick, intelligent creatures, able to move easily through the ocean.

Jet Propulsion

Octopuses, squids, and nautiluses share a unique way of traveling through the ocean. They use jet propulsion to get from place to place. First, they suck in a great deal of water. Then, they quickly squirt the water out. The pressure from releasing the water moves these cephalopods through the ocean!

SOFT BODIES

There are no bones in the soft body of a giant Pacific octopus. Because of this, the octopus is able to squeeze into tight, tiny spaces despite its huge size!

Giant Pacific Octopus

Length: 25 feet from tentacle to tentacle

Weight: up to 400 pounds

Diet: crabs, snails, clams, fish

Range: Pacific Ocean

Giant Pacific octopuses make their homes on the sea floor, up to 2,500 feet deep. These intelligent mollusks are able to hide in plain sight. Special cells in their skin allow octopuses to change their skin color. The octopuses also change the texture of their skin. In an instant, the octopus can blend in with coral, rocks, or the ocean floor. Neither predators nor prey can spot this octopus easily if it lurks nearby!

Prehistoric relatives of today's squid and cuttlefish, belemnites were ancient cephalopods. Scientists believe they roamed the oceans of the Triassic, Jurassic, and Cretaceous periods, dying out around the same time as the dinosaurs. Many belemnite fossils preserved the animal's hard skeleton. It was long and round, shaped similar to a cigar. Fewer fossils show the structure of belemnites' soft parts. But based on fossil evidence, scientists believe that, like modern squids and octopuses, belemnites were equipped with ink sacs. They may have sprayed predators with ink to get away!

BIG-EYED BEASTS

The eyes of a giant squid may reach 1 foot across. No other animal has eyes so large! A giant squid's eyes can take in a lot of light, even at depths where little light reaches. This helps the squid spot prey and predators in dim waters.

Giant Squid

Length: up to 43 feet

Weight: up to 2,000 pounds

Diet: fish, other squids

Range: Atlantic Ocean, Indian Ocean, Pacific Ocean

Eight arms hang down from the body of a giant squid. Beyond them stretch two long feeding tentacles. Their length makes giant squids fearsome predators, able to seize prey even from a distance of 30 feet! A sharp beak nestles between the giant squid's arms. Inside, the squid's teeth tear apart the cephalopod's prey.

Chambered Nautilus

Size: up to 8 inches across

Diet: crustaceans, fish

Range: Eastern Indian Ocean, Western Pacific Ocean

A shell encases a nautilus's body, protecting the nautilus from predators. The shell is divided into gas-filled chambers. As the nautilus ages, its shell grows more chambers. These gas-filled chambers allow the nautilus to control whether it floats or sinks. At night, the chambered nautilus hunts near coral reefs. But during the day, it sinks into water as deep as 2,000 feet. Deeper waters provide protection from predators. But a nautilus must be careful not to drift too deep. The deeper it goes, the more the pressure from water above increases. If the pressure becomes too much, it will crush the nautilus's shell!

Dolphins and Whales
of the Open Ocean

Swimming through the open ocean, dolphins and whales may look like fish, but they are actually marine mammals. Marine mammals are some of the most intelligent animals in the ocean. And whales are among the largest.

Up for Air

Dolphins and whales do not have gills like fish. They cannot breathe underwater. Instead, they must return to the surface whenever they need to breathe. Nostrils called blowholes sit on top of their heads. Tight flaps cover the blowholes when they are underwater. But at the surface, dolphins and whales open their blowholes to breathe deep before diving again.

HUNTING TOOLS

In western Australia, some bottlenose dolphins use tools while they hunt. As they search for food along the seafloor, dolphins sometimes hold a sea sponge in their beaks. This protects their snout from sharp rocks and coral while hunting!

Bottlenose Dolphin

Length: up to 12.5 feet

Weight: up to 1,400 pounds

Diet: fish, crustaceans, squid

Range: Atlantic Ocean, Indian Ocean, Pacific Ocean

Dolphins are social creatures. They slap their tails, chirp, click, and whistle to communicate with others. These smart, playful animals often swim together in groups. Usually, their pods have no more than 20 dolphins. But sometimes, more than 1,000 dolphins can join together!

For many years, scientists knew that whales likely evolved from four-legged land mammals. In 1994, paleontologists finally dug up the link between the two: the *Ambulocetus natans* ("walking swimming whale"). It had lived in shallow seas that covered Pakistan about 49 million years ago. True to its name, the *Ambulocetus* was able to move both on land and in water. At about 10 feet long, the *Ambulocetus* had four strong limbs. Each limb had long fingers or toes that were likely webbed. Paleontologists believe the *Ambulocetus* likely lived along ocean shores, waiting motionlessly to ambush unsuspecting prey.

Blue Whale

Length: up to 110 feet

Weight: up to 330,000 pounds

Diet: krill

Range: Arctic Ocean, Atlantic Ocean, Indian Ocean, Pacific Ocean, Southern Ocean

Blue whales are not just the largest animals on Earth today; scientists believe they are the largest animals to have ever lived! They grow this large eating some of the smallest animals in the ocean: krill. Instead of teeth, blue whales have fringed plates called **baleen**. The baleen works like a feeding filter. Blue whales open their mouths wide to pull in ocean water and any tiny animals in it. Then, they force the water back out through the **baleen** plates. Water passes through the baleen, but krill and other small animals cannot. These creatures become the blue whale's dinner!

Orca

Length: up to 32 feet

Weight: up to 22,000 pounds

Diet: fish, squid, seals, sharks

Range: Arctic Ocean, Atlantic Ocean, Indian Ocean, Pacific Ocean, Southern Ocean

Able to swim at 30 miles per hour and sporting 3-inch teeth, orcas are fearsome predators. Up to 15 form pods that travel and hunt together. A pod of orcas may surround a school of small fish, slapping the fish to stun and eat them. Sometimes orcas prey upon seals sitting on ice floes. The orcas make waves that wash the seal into the ocean, where they catch and devour it. Orcas have even been known to defeat great white sharks!

Sharks
of the Open Ocean

The open ocean is known to hold some of the ocean's most fearsome fish: sharks. More than 400 different species of sharks swim in ocean waters, from its deepest depths to its shallow coasts. Yet not all sharks are fierce predators. Some scavenge for their food, while others are peaceful filter feeders.

TOOTHY MOUTHS

Rows of sharp teeth fill the mouths of many sharks. Great white sharks always have about 300 teeth in their mouths at once. If one falls out, a new tooth grows in its place. Thousands of teeth may pass through a single shark's mouth during its lifetime.

Something Fishy

As fish, sharks have gills to take in oxygen from ocean waters. Fins propel them through the ocean. They move their bodies from side to side to swim. But a shark's skeleton is different from that of many other fish. It is made of flexible **cartilage** instead of hard bone.

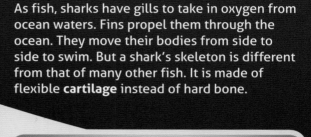

Tooth Fossils

Since prehistoric times, sharks have been constantly shedding and replacing teeth. These hard teeth are more likely to become fossilized than sharks' relatively soft cartilaginous skeletons. Sometimes, fossilized shark teeth wash ashore. But paleontologists also dig fossilized shark teeth from sedimentary rock!

Whale Shark

Length: up to 65 feet
Weight: 26,000 pounds
Diet: small fish, plankton
Range: Atlantic Ocean, Indian Ocean, Pacific Ocean

Whale sharks are the largest fish in the ocean! They are gentle giants, slowly swimming through the ocean. They spread open their 5-foot-wide mouths to suck in water. After, they force the water out over their gills, trapping plankton and small fish within their mouths. Then, they feast!

About 28 million years ago, the *Carcharocles megalodon* swam Earth's oceans. Paleontologists best know this animal from the fossilized teeth it left behind. An ancient ancestor of today's great white shark, this prehistoric giant ruled the seas until about 2.6 million years ago. Some *Carcharocles megalodon* teeth are 7.6 inches long! From this tooth size, paleontologists estimate that the shark could have been as long as 52 feet. No other fish in history has ever been so large!

Great White Shark

Length: up to 20 feet

Weight: up to 5,000 pounds

Diet: seals, sea lions, small whales, dolphins, tunas

Range: Atlantic Ocean, Indian Ocean, Pacific Ocean

Great white sharks are powerful, aggressive predators. They are at the top of the ocean's food chain. Few other ocean creatures threaten this fierce fish. An incredible sense of smell leads great white sharks to prey. They can smell blood from a distance of 3 miles! Reaching 3 inches long, the teeth of a great white shark have **serrated** edges to tear into their prey's flesh!

Tiger Shark

Length: 18 feet

Weight: 2,000 pounds

Diet: fish, sea turtles, seals, dolphins, jellyfish

Range: Atlantic Ocean, Indian Ocean, Pacific Ocean

Stripes cross the bodies of young tiger sharks, giving these fish their name. Tiger sharks are ferocious sharks that often swim in coastal waters. Their sharp, serrated teeth can rip through the tough shells of sea turtles!

The Ocean Depths

Life in the deep ocean is extreme. It is constantly in pitch-black darkness. Temperatures sit just above freezing. Immense pressure from the thousands of feet of water above press down on the creatures that live there. Food can be hard to come by. It seems impossible to believe that animals could live in this habitat. But the deep ocean is home to a diverse blend of creatures. With transparent bodies, massive eyes, and the ability to glow, these creatures of the deep have developed unique adaptations to survive.

LIFE OF THE HOT SPRINGS

Scientists first discovered deep-sea vents in 1977. They were also surprised to find living creatures nearby! Previously unknown species of clams, mussels, crabs, fish, and worms all thrived in this dark, extreme environment. The water from the vents was rich in minerals, supporting a great diversity of life!

Marine Snow

In the ocean, snow is not a weather phenomenon. Rather, marine snow is tiny particles of matter. It is made up of organic material, such as decaying animals and plants, and droppings from ocean animals. The marine snow drifts down through the upper layers of the ocean to reach the ocean depths.

As they sink, the tiny pieces of marine snow latch together. They may form "flakes" a few centimeters across. The larger they grow, the faster they fall. Still, marine snow has a long journey to the bottom of the ocean. Scientists estimate that it takes weeks for a flake to reach the seafloor.

Many animals in the ocean depths rely on marine snow for food. They eat the gradually sinking "flakes" as they drift past toward the ocean floor.

Vampire Squid

Size: up to 15 inches long

Diet: marine snow

Range: Atlantic Ocean, Pacific Ocean, Indian Ocean

The vampire squid survives on marine snow. Along with eight webbed legs, this cephalopod has two long filaments. With these filaments, the creatures fish for marine snow. Mucus helps the squid collect flakes from the water around it. Then, the squid wraps the flakes in mucus, forming a ball of food and mucus that the squid then eats. Vampire squids use their **bioluminescent** mucus to confuse and distract predators!

Dumbo Octopus

Size: up to 6 feet long

Diet: snails, worms

Range: Atlantic Ocean, Indian Ocean, Pacific Ocean

Two fins stand out from either side of a Dumbo octopus's mantle. At least fifteen species of Dumbo octopus dwell in the ocean depths. They can be found as deep as 14,800 feet below the water's surface. Most species are small, no larger than 12 inches long. Dumbo octopuses can move in a variety of ways. They may crawl on the seafloor, use jet propulsion, or flap their fins.

Animals
of the Deep Ocean

The secrets of the deep ocean are largely unknown. It is hard to study the animals of this vast, dark area. And humans have only explored less than 5 percent of it. With each year that passes, scientists continue to discover previously unknown deep-sea species!

DEEP-SEA CORAL

Coral does not only appear in shallow, tropical waters. Scientists have found coral living in the cold, dark waters of the deep ocean, almost 20,000 feet below the ocean's surface. Some of these corals are more than 4,000 years old!

Bioluminescence

Sunlight cannot reach the deep ocean. Still, a trip to the ocean depths could be a bright experience. Some deep-ocean animals have the ability to sparkle and glow in the dark. They make their own light! This is called bioluminescence.

For some creatures, bioluminescence helps them to find mates. Other creatures have found it helps defend against predators. Still others use it to draw in unsuspecting prey!

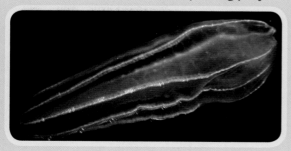

Fangtooth Fish

Size: up to 6 inches long

Diet: fish, crustaceans, squid

Range: Atlantic Ocean, Indian Ocean, Pacific Ocean

Fangtooth fish are named for their huge teeth. A special adaptation helps the fangtooth close its mouth. When its mouth is closed, the fangtooth's lower fangs fit into special pockets on the roof of its mouth. This protects the fish's brain from the sharp teeth. Without this adaptation, a fangtooth's teeth would stab into its brain! Fangtooth fish spend their days deep in the ocean, at depths reaching 16,404 feet. But at night, they migrate closer to the ocean's surface. There, they feed on fish and other prey, trapping them in their formidable teeth.

Along for the Ride

A female humpback anglerfish is much larger than a male. A male anglerfish uses its strong sense of smell to sniff out a female mate. Then, it latches on to the female's underside. Later, the male separates from the female once it has fertilized her eggs.

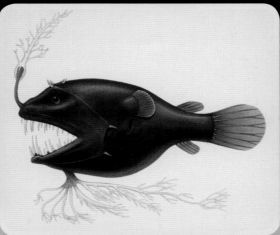

Goblin Shark

Length: up to 12.75 feet

Weight: up to 460 pounds

Diet: squid, crustaceans, fish

Range: Atlantic Ocean, Indian Ocean, Pacific Ocean

Sensors line the goblin shark's long, distinctive snout. These help the goblin shark detect prey along the dark ocean floor. The shark's unique jaw is able to change positions. The jaw can move forward to capture prey! Then, the goblin shark pulls its jaw back to its original position. Sharp, spiny teeth line the goblin shark's mouth.

Humpback Anglerfish

Size: Females: up to 6 inches; Males: up to 1.1 inches

Diet: fish

Range: Atlantic Ocean, Indian Ocean, Pacific Ocean

A barb stands from the head of a female humpback anglerfish. It projects from her head like a fishing pole. A glowing bulb at the barb's end lures in prey. Once the prey draws close, the anglerfish opens her mouth, which is filled with sharp, fanglike teeth. A broad mouth means that the anglerfish can eat prey twice her size!

The Health of the Oceans

Colorful, unique, and vibrant life fills the oceans. Yet these ocean treasures face many threats. Climate change, pollution, and more jeopardize the health of Earth's oceans and ocean life. Many of these threats result from human actions. It is important that humans work to protect the oceans.

Climate Change

Scientists know that Earth's climate naturally goes through cycles. Sometimes, the planet is very hot, while other times it is frozen in an ice age. Yet scientists have noticed that certain human activities impact the planet's climate, causing global warming.

So far, global warming has caused Earth's temperature to rise by about 2 degrees Fahrenheit. It may seem minor, but those few degrees have a huge impact. Ice sheets are melting. The sea level is rising. The oceans are warming. Storms are growing more powerful and violent. All of these effects are harmful to life in the oceans.

Coral Bleaching

Already coral reefs are feeling the effects of climate change. Recently, some have experienced coral bleaching. Many believe this is because of warming ocean waters and pollution, which place coral under stress. When stressed, coral forces zooxanthellae out, eventually leading to the coral's death. Without the zooxanthellae to provide color, the coral appears white like its skeleton.

Melting Ice

Polar bears rely on sea ice for survival. They build their dens and hunt for food from the ice. But as the ice melts, polar bears lose their homes and access to food. Climate change threatens polar bears with extinction.

GARBAGE

About 1.4 billion pounds of garbage reaches the oceans each year. Some of it washes to shore, while some sinks to the ocean floor. And some is swept out to sea by the currents, forming vast "garbage patches" in the open ocean. Studies show that tiger sharks often eat plastic, metal, and other garbage in the ocean. Sea turtles confuse plastic bags for their jellyfish prey. Fishing nets ensnare whales, seals, and other ocean animals.

What Can Humans Do?

Climate change and pollution have already impacted the ocean. But humans can still take action to protect the ocean's treasures.

Drive less, use public transportation, bicycle, and carpool. Gas-powered vehicles release carbon dioxide into the atmosphere. Scientists have linked an increase in carbon dioxide in the atmosphere to climate change.

Recycle items rather than throwing them away. Producing less garbage means less garbage reaches the oceans and threatens marine life.

Take a trip to the beach and pick up garbage along the shores. Even cleaning up around your local lake or river—which eventually drain to the ocean—can help keep the ocean clean. It's up to humans to keep our oceans clean and protect all the treasures Earth's oceans have to offer.

Dead Zones

When it rains, rainwater carries fertilizers and other chemicals into nearby rivers. Rivers then wash those chemicals into the oceans. The chemicals stimulate the growth of algae, which ultimately limits the amount of oxygen in the water. Without enough oxygen, marine creatures die or flee. This creates areas known as "dead zones" where polluted rivers and oceans meet.

Quiz

1 Walruses, seals, and sea lions are all known as _____. This word means "flipper-footed"!

a) corals
b) bivalves
c) pinnipeds

2 Periwinkle snails are part of the mollusk family. What body part do periwinkles use to move around?

a) leg
b) foot
c) arm

3 Mary Anning was an accomplished fossil hunter in the 1800s. What long-necked marine reptile did Mary Anning discover?

a) plesiosaur
b) placoderm
c) Wiwaxia

4 Earth's five oceans hold 97 percent of Earth's water. Which ocean is the largest?

a) Atlantic Ocean
b) Southern Ocean
c) Pacific Ocean

5 Walruses dive down to the seafloor to search for food. What body part helps walruses sense clams and other food on the ocean floor?

a) whiskers
b) flippers
c) tusks

6

What is marine snow?

a) falling pieces of organic particles
b) a weather phenomenon
c) a disease

7

The deepest point in the ocean is nearly 7 miles below the ocean's surface. What is the name of this spot?

a) Mid-Atlantic Ridge
b) Great Barrier Reef
c) Challenger Deep

8

The pull of the Moon's gravity causes the tides. How often do the coasts see high tide?

a) twice a day
b) twice a week
c) twice a month

9
The stinging tentacles of a sea anemone scare many creatures away. Yet what animal makes its home among sea anemones?

a) lionfish
b) peacock mantis shrimp
c) clown anemonefish

10

For many marine animals, camouflage is key to survival. Which of the following is a way camouflage helps animals?

a) hides the animal from predators
b) hides the animal while it hunts
c) both a & b

Glossary

arthropod: an invertbrate animal such as insects, spiders, and crustaceans

baleen: fringed plates in the mouths of some whales that are used to filter out food from water

bioluminescence: an animal's ability to make its own light

camouflage: coloring and texture of a creature that allows it to blend in with its surroundings

cartilage: flexible tissue

climate: the average weather conditions in a place over a long time

evolve: to slowly grow and change over a very long period of time

extinct: to die out completely, to no longer exist

fossils: preserved remains of long-dead plants and animals

habitat: type of environment where an organism usually lives

invertebrate: an animal without a backbone

magma: hot, molten rock under Earth's crust

migrate: to move from one place to another

nematocyst: a stinging cell

organism: a living thing, such as a plant or animal

paleontologist: a scientist who examines fossils to learn more about past periods in Earth's history

photosynthesis: a process when a plant uses energy from the Sun to make its food

plankton: the abundant organisms that drift through the ocean on currents; zooplankton are drifting animals, while phytoplankton are plants

predator: an animal that hunts other animals for food

prey: an animal that is hunted by another animal for food

reptile: an animal that is cold-blooded, lays eggs, and is covered in scales

serrated: having a jagged edge

suspension feeder: a creature that remains in one place and waits for food in the water to drift past

tectonic plates: moving slabs of the Earth's crust

tentacle: a flexible body part attached to the head or mouth of an animal, such as an octopus or anemone, that can be used for grabbing, feeling, or moving

Excavation Instructions

The box in the front of the kit includes an excavation brick and two tools.

1 Begin by laying out a piece of newspaper or paper to excavate on. Place the brick on the sheet of paper.

2 Take the pick and begin scraping away the dirt. It's helpful to begin at one edge and work inward.

3 Once an artifact is discovered, use the brush tool to sweep away the debris.

4 Continue excavating until all four artifacts are excavated.